MY EXPERIMENTS WITH TRUTH

WITH TRUTH

MAHATMA GANDHI

MY EXPERIMENTS WITH TRUTH

MAHATMA GANDHI

www.realreads.co.uk

Retold by Nandini Nayar
Illustrated by Shailja Jain Chougule

Published by Real Reads Ltd
Stroud, Gloucestershire, UK
www.realreads.co.uk

Text copyright © DC Books, 2015
Illustrations copyright © DC Books, 2015
Published in conjunction with DC Books, Kottayam, Kerala, India

First published in 2015

ISBN 978-1-906230-88-3

Printed in China by Wai Man Book Binding (China) Ltd
Designed by Lucy Guenot
Typeset by Bookcraft Ltd, Stroud, Gloucestershire

CONTENTS

THE CHARACTERS

Mohandas Karamchand 'Mahatma' Gandhi

Gandhi's education in England and experiences in South Africa have led him to question the values and beliefs he grew up with in India. Will he be able to help lead his people to freedom?

Kasturbai Gandhi

Married to Mohandas at a young age, Kasturbai is his companion and student. Can she maintain her independence while supporting her demanding husband?

Putlibai

Mohandas's mother, well known for her generosity and patience, sets an example to her children which can be hard to follow. Will Mohandas be able to keep his promises to her?

4

Karamchand Gandhi

His father's calm acceptance of the pain of his illness impresses Gandhi. Will he be able to fulfil his father's expectations?

Gopal Krishna Gokhale

An important member of the Indian National Congress, Gokhale dreams of independence for India. Will his dreams be fulfilled?

Abdulla Sheth

As an Indian businessman in South Africa, Abdulla has learnt to accept discrimination against Indians. Will his support of Gandhi help his community?

MY EXPERIMENTS WITH TRUTH

Our family, the Gandhis, are Hindus belonging
to the Bania caste, which consists largely of
merchants, spice dealers, money-lenders and
bankers. The menfolk of the Bania traditionally
held important government posts. My
grandfather was the Prime Minister of Kathiawad
in Gujarat, a western state of India, while my
father, Karamchand Gandhi, was the Prime
Minister of Rajkot. My father was an honest and
fearless man. My mother, Putlibai, my father's
fourth and last wife, was a very devout woman.
Together they had a daughter and three sons.
I was their youngest son, born in the Indian
coastal city of Porbandar, on October 2nd 1869.

When I was seven we moved to Rajkot, where
I continued my schooling. I was a good student
but I was very shy, running home after school to
avoid talking to my classmates. One day at school
there was great excitement. Mr Giles, who was
the state Education Minister, was inspecting our

high school. In order to test our class he said he would give us five English words to spell, which we had to write on our slates. When I had finished I felt someone nudge my foot. I looked up and saw that it was our teacher, who was quietly encouraging me to copy from my neighbour. It was obvious that I had made a mistake, but I wasn't willing to copy. Mr Giles checked our slates. 'Only Gandhi has got a word wrong. Gandhi,' he glowered, 'you got *kettle* wrong!' The teacher glared at me, and I knew I had failed him, but I was happy that I had not cheated.

During my childhood, there were two stories which greatly influenced me. One was the story of Shravan, who was renowned for his devotion to his parents. This inspired me to serve my own parents as well as I could. The second was the story of Harishchandra, a noble king of ancient India. Harishchandra was pious and just, never breaking a promise. His story made me wonder why we couldn't all be as truthful as he was.

When I was thirteen, I married a beautiful woman called Kasturbai. I am afraid I was a possessive husband, and my attempts to control Kasturbai led to frequent quarrels.

In my early teens, cricket and gymnastics were made compulsory at school. Although I was not fond of physical exercise I always attended these sessions. One Saturday I miscalculated the time and arrived late. I was fined for being late, but what hurt me the most was that the principal refused to believe that I had just misread the clock. I realised then that if I wanted to be accepted as a truthful person, I must accept that people will sometimes insist on their own truths. But in the matter of handwriting I am afraid I *was* careless. All attempts to improve later in life were unsuccessful, and to this day I regret not having good handwriting.

'Mohan,' my mother said to me one day, 'I am afraid you have fallen into bad company!'

I knew she was referring to the friendship I had developed with my elder brother's best friend, and I knew that it was because this boy ate meat, which was against our Hindu religion. 'Don't worry,' I told my mother, 'I am going to reform him!'

So when I next met the boy, I asked him why it was important for him to eat meat.

'Haven't you heard the rhyme?' he asked.

'What rhyme?'

'The one that goes: "Behold the mighty Englishman, he rules the Indian small; because he is a meat-eater he is five cubits tall."'

I decided that I too wanted to be as strong and brave as an Englishman so I could stop being afraid of the dark. Our maid Rambha had taught me to say 'Rama, Rama' to ward off the fear, but I was still afraid of the dark, so I gave in to temptation and started eating meat. I didn't enjoy it much, and was haunted by imagining the goat bleating piteously, but my friend refused to let me stop. Soon I was eating meat regularly, even though it meant hiding it from my parents and lying to my mother. I felt very guilty, and after a year I gave it up. I've never gone back to eating meat.

About this time I also committed the crime of stealing. In order to help my elder brother to pay off a debt I cut off a section of his gold armlet without telling anyone and sold it. My guilty conscience would not let me rest. I decided to confess, and wrote a letter to my father telling him what I had done. My father wept as he read it, but I knew I was forgiven. I loved my father, and took pleasure in serving him during his illness. I was devastated when he died.

In 1887 I finished my schooling. A family friend suggested going to England for higher education, even though the headman of our caste thought that it was wrong for members of the caste to travel abroad. My mother was reluctant to let me go.

'I have heard how young men change once they cross the seas,' she told me.

'I vow not to touch wine, women and meat,' I said. My promise relieved my mother, and she gave me her blessing. I left for Bombay with a light heart, bidding farewell to my wife Kasturbai and our small son. Bad news awaited me in Bombay. The sea was too rough to travel, forcing me to wait several days, and I finally sailed from Bombay on September 4th. For disobeying the headman of my caste and daring to cross the sea, I was declared an outcast by some people.

I was too shy to speak English, and so was very lonely on the voyage. Uncertain of which food was vegetarian, I practically starved, eating only the food I had brought with me. At Southampton I met Dr Mehta, who gave me my first lessons in British etiquette, warning me not to do many of the things that Indians usually did. I was miserable in England, missing my mother and home. I hated the tasteless vegetarian food, and felt too much of an outsider to be comfortable.

I made attempts to change myself to suit my new surroundings, buying new clothes, and enrolling in dance and violin classes, but I soon realised the insignificance of these things and gave them up. I maintained a strict account of my expenses, a habit that helped me later in life. I simplified my life by living in one room and cooking my own breakfast. This gave me the time to prepare for the matriculation examination, and after intensive study I passed. None of this cured me of my shyness, however, and I still found myself unable to speak to people. I could not deliver a speech even if I had a prepared script with me. Although I overcame this shyness later in life, it instilled in me the habit of choosing my words with great care. My time in England presented me with several opportunities to tell untruths, but each time I managed to overcome the temptation.

In order to practise law as a barrister, or be 'called to bar', a student had to pass all their law examinations and 'keep terms', which meant attending at least six dinners each term. In the past the purpose of these dinners would have been to allow the students to get the opportunity to listen to experts' speeches and express their own views. By the time I was studying as a barrister, however, there were far too many students, and we were seated at a separate table, away from the experts.

Although most students did not study for the exams, I read all the books. That helped me to pass the exams, and I was called to the bar on June 10th 1891. On June 11th I enrolled in the High Court, and on the 12th I sailed home. As the great ship carried me home to India I was prey to many doubts and fears. I was filled with textbook knowledge, but what did I know of practical cases?

My brother greeted me in Bombay with the sad news that our mother had died while I was in England. I went for a traditional cleansing swim in the river at Nasik. Many members of my community still considered me an outcast, yet my calm acceptance of their opinions gradually won them over, and many of them helped me later in my life.

I moved to Bombay, the most populous city in India, hoping to learn something from observing cases in the High Court, but I usually dozed off in the courtroom and so learnt nothing at all! When I had the opportunity to take on a legal case, my fear of speaking in public was so great that I had to refuse it. I went back to Rajkot, and for a while earned a living writing petitions. I was then offered a job to assist in a legal case in South Africa at one hundred and five pounds a year; I agreed immediately, eager to see a new country. I bade goodbye to my family and set sail in April 1893, reaching the port of Durban at the end of May.

In Durban I met the businessman Abdulla Sheth, who accompanied me to the courthouse. The magistrate stared at my clothes and asked me to take off my turban. I realised then that many battles awaited me in South Africa. My fight began with letters to the newspapers, describing the turban incident. I soon learnt that Indians were called 'coolies', and I was a 'coolie barrister'. I realised that the Asians in South Africa were not held in much respect.

When I travelled to South Africa's northern city of Pretoria to prepare for Abdulla Sheth's case I decided to travel first class. That evening the train stopped at Maritzburg, the capital of Natal. A passenger who got into the compartment informed the officials that a 'coloured man' was travelling first class.

'You cannot travel first class,' I was told.

'But I have a first class ticket,' I protested.

'Get out!' the official said, 'or I will get a constable to push you out!'

'Do that,' I told him. 'I will not get off this train!' A constable pushed me and my luggage out of the train. I refused to board the second class carriage, and stood on the platform, watching the train disappear. I spent the night in the waiting room, shivering in the cold because my overcoat was in the bag that the authorities had taken away.

Should I stay in South Africa and fight? Going back to India seemed like cowardice. I decided to stay, and took the next train.

On the stagecoach from Charleston to Johannesburg I was insulted again. I was given the coachman's seat outside the coach, since it was considered inappropriate for me to sit inside with the white passengers. By now my only desire was to reach my destination, so I swallowed this insult, but when the coachman said, 'Sami, off that seat! You sit on the footboard!' I could not bear it any longer. 'You gave me this seat,' I retorted. 'I will only move if you let me sit inside the coach.' The coachman began to beat me and tried to drag me from my seat. I clung stubbornly to the rails, determined not to give up. The beating ended only when the other passengers stopped the coachman, and they allowed me to sit inside the coach. I wrote to the coach company, demanding a seat inside the coach for the next stage of my journey; my seat on the coach to Johannesburg the next day was inside.

My host, Abdul Gani Sheth, listened to my experiences and said, 'Only Indians can live in a country like this because we are prepared to put up with insults to earn our keep.'

'I don't believe you have tried hard enough to fight these unfair rules,' I replied.

I was certain that clothes would make a difference to the treatment meted out to me, so I dressed in 'correct' English clothes. The next time I travelled first class to Pretoria the guard again tried to throw me out, but was stopped by the only other passenger.

In Pretoria I was given a room in a hotel on the condition that I would eat in my own room, so the Europeans would not be offended eating beside me, but the owner of the hotel was a good man who was disturbed by his own request. 'Do please eat in the dining room,' he said. 'I have spoken to the other guests, and none of them object to your presence.'

Indians were not allowed to walk on public footpaths, and had to be indoors before 9 pm.

Although I had a letter permitting me to be out after this time, a guard once kicked me off the footpath. My friend saw this and offered to be my witness if I took the case to court. 'No, no,' I said. 'It is my rule not to go to court over my personal problems.'

My experiences made me determined to speak to the Indian community about conditions in Pretoria, and it was at such a meeting that I gave my first public speech. I urged the Indians to be truthful in their business transactions, reminding them that they were representatives of their country here. I suggested establishing an association to represent our problems to the authorities. My speech drew a positive response.

The case I had come to South Africa to represent gave me an opportunity to learn by observing the lawyers working on it. I realised that when truth is on our side, the law can help us. Truth was on the side of my client, Abdulla Sheth, and he was sure to win, but his opponent would be hit hard by the defeat. I suggested that the two parties settle the case between themselves; they accepted and soon the case was satisfactorily resolved.

My work done, I returned to Durban and prepared for the journey home.

At the farewell party given in my honour, I happened to read about the law that was trying to deprive Indians of their right to elect members of the Natal Legislative Assembly.

'How can such a law be passed?' I asked Abdulla Sheth.

'We are seen as uneducated men who know only our own business,' he answered.

'But don't you see?' I protested, 'if this law is passed, life will become very difficult for us!'

'Then why don't you cancel your ticket, stay on in South Africa, and help us?' suggested one of the guests.

'Yes,' Abdulla Sheth agreed. 'Just tell us what you will charge us.'

'I do not require any fee,' I told them, 'but this fight will require funds.'

And in this manner, the farewell marked the beginning of a new phase in my life.

I was soon busy with meetings to draw up a petition to submit to the Legislative Assembly. The law depriving Indians of the right to vote was passed, but I was not disheartened, as the struggle had brought the Indian community together and helped them realise they had to fight for their rights. The Indian community was unwilling to let me leave. 'I will stay,' I told them, 'but only if I can live independently and not rely on public funds.'

I settled down in Natal, assured of work from a number of Indian merchants. I applied for membership of the Natal Supreme Court. Although the Law Society objected to my application since I was not a European, I was granted membership. Since I had to adopt the court's dress code I had to give up my turban.

'Why did you give up your turban without a fight?' my friends asked.

'I do not want to waste my skills fighting petty battles,' I explained, 'I want to fight the bigger battle for equality.'

A Natal Indian Congress was set up and attracted many members, but poor Indians, the indentured labourers, could not afford the subscription.

I helped a labourer named Balasundaram, who had been beaten by his master and whose story had spread far and wide. This brought other labourers into my office and gave me an opportunity to learn more about their troubles.

My work went so well that the next three years in South Africa passed quickly and I was never short of work. In 1896 I went home to India for a few months and continued my work there, writing a pamphlet about the condition of the Indians in South Africa. This pamphlet attracted a lot of attention, and I travelled to Bombay and Madras to meet important people and express my views. My work was interrupted by a telegram from Natal, asking me to return, so towards the end of that year I set off again for South Africa, this time with my wife, my two sons, and my sister's son.

On the ship I had reason to be proud of my family, all dressed in the Parsi style. At that time I believed that only European clothes helped us look civilised, though I soon lost my fascination for stylish clothes.

When we reached Durban after eighteen days at sea, we were in for a shock. Our ship was not allowed to dock. 'Why are we not allowed to get off the ship?' Kasturbai asked me.

'The Europeans have accused me of criticising them,' I explained, 'and of bringing a ship load of Indians to settle in Natal.'

When the ship was finally allowed to dock, my family was taken away to safety and I was asked to enter the city at night. Despite these precautions I was attacked. I was saved when a lady came between me and the mob, and managed to reach my friend's house. I was assured that if I identified the men who had attacked me, they would be punished, but I refused to do this because I was sure that they had been misled. I made it clear that my speeches in India had contained no inflammatory statements, and along with my refusal to punish my attackers this helped people recognise that I was innocent. This gave the Indian community in South Africa a lot of attention, and the Europeans realised that Indians would fight for their rights.

Although I was busy with public work I found the time to settle my family in their new home. We had little money, and our home life changed from a relatively luxurious one to one that was more simple. I cut down my expenses by doing as much as possible myself. First I learnt to starch my collars for my appearances in court.

'Gandhi,' my friends said when they saw me, 'your collar is dripping!'

'This is the first collar I have starched,' I explained.

'Why don't you get it done by the laundry?' they asked.

I explained to them that I liked doing these things. 'Not only am I saving money,' I said, 'but I have entertained you too.'

There was fresh laughter when I appeared in court with my self-cut hair. 'The rats have been nibbling at your hair!' my friends teased me.

In time I became an expert at both starching clothes and cutting hair.

My reforms were not restricted to myself, but aimed too at the Indian community. I wanted my countrymen to understand the importance of looking after themselves and taking pride in their culture. My actions also had a positive impact on the Europeans, who appreciated my eagerness to encourage my Indian countrymen.

Although I was happy with my work, I longed to return to India. The Indian community was shocked to hear this, but once they realised that I was determined, they honoured me with expensive gifts. I wanted to leave the gifts for the Indians in Durban, but Kasturbai was not happy with my decision. 'They belong to us,' she said.

'How can we own such expensive things when we are trying to simplify our lives?' I asked.

The argument raged for some time, but my wife finally agreed with my point of view and the gifts were given away.

In 1901 I travelled to India again, to participate in the Indian National Congress in Calcutta, and present the facts about the situation of Indians in South Africa. The camp where the delegates were put up shocked me; there were very few bathroom facilities, and the volunteers were treated very much as second class citizens. I presented my resolution in one of the Congress sessions, and it was passed without anyone having read or understood it. This saddened me. Would those in charge in India ever understand the plight of Indians in South Africa? I consoled myself with the thought that the passing of the resolution by the Congress at least meant that it had the tacit approval of the nation.

After the Congress I stayed on in Calcutta
with the radical politician and social reformer
Gopal Krishna Gokhale. 'You cannot afford to
be so shy and reserved!' Gokhale scolded me.
'You must meet more people!'

Gokhale treated me like a brother, and introduced me to several important people in Calcutta. Gokhale's dream was the freedom of our country.

I visited the famous Kali temple, and was shocked to see rivers of blood from the sheep being sacrificed there. Though I was assured that the sheep felt nothing, Hindus believe that an animal's life is as important as that of a human being, and I resolved that animal sacrifice must be stopped.

From Calcutta I set out on a tour of India. I decided to travel by third class so that I could experience at first hand the hardships of the common people. My travels in third class compartments made me realise that the authorities were indifferent to the fate of people travelling in this class, but I was also aware that the passengers were themselves responsible for turning these compartments into dirty, noisy places.

It was Gokhale's wish that I settle in Bombay
so I could help him, but I was reluctant to go
back to Bombay when I had failed there before.
Instead, I began to work in Rajkot. It was only
after I tasted success in my work here that I
decided to move to Bombay.

One day Kasturbai came to me with some
disturbing news. 'Manilal is ill,' she said.

It soon became clear that my second son
Manilal was suffering from typhoid. The doctor
suggested feeding him eggs and chicken.

'Manilal,' I said to him, 'the doctor has suggested eggs and chicken, but I have decided to try some treatment of my own.'

'I am glad,' replied Manilal. 'I will not eat eggs or chicken.'

My treatment worked, and Manilal's fever broke. My worries about my son at rest, I turned back to work.

One day I received a telegram informing me that Joseph Chamberlain, the British Colonial Secretary, was expected in South Africa, and that I was needed there. I was reluctant to leave Bombay when we had just settled there, but I knew that my South African friends needed me and I prepared to set sail. As soon as I reached my destination I set to work to write out the petition to be submitted to Mr Chamberlain.

When the group of Indian representatives eventually met Mr Chamberlain we were given a negative response. He was not willing to speak up in favour of the Indians since this would annoy the whites.

During this time the Hindu text *Bhagavad Gita*, which preaches selfless action, became my guide. I decided to stop sending money to my family and use it instead to help the needy; this upset my brother, who had spent a lot of money and effort on my education. My diet too changed; I gave up milk entirely and lived on a diet of fruits and nuts.

The end of the Boer War in May 1902 made it necessary for people to get permits to go to the South African province of Transvaal. The officers in charge of permits were corrupt, and Indians came to me every day with fresh complaints. 'The officers denied me a permit to enter Transvaal,' they told me, 'yet someone else was given one on payment of a hundred pounds!' I enrolled in the Transvaal Supreme Court, set up an office in Johannesburg, and collected evidence against two of the officers.

It was hard to get the court to act on the complaint of a coloured man against a white man, and although the guilt of the two men was obvious they were let off. They were, however, removed from their jobs, and this made the Indians happy. Personally I had nothing against the two men; I had learnt that one should hate the sin but not the sinner.

In 1904 *Indian Opinion* was launched, a magazine to discuss the issues affecting Indians in South Africa. I wrote extensively for *Indian Opinion*, keeping the people in India up to date with developments in South Africa.

At this time I was working on behalf of a number of poor Indians in Johannesburg, who were seeking rights over the land where they were living. I took on several cases and won practically all of them. Eventually the municipality acquired the land, and when there was an outbreak of plague my friends and I nursed the Indians who fell ill, and encouraged the municipality to take prompt action to improve sanitation facilities.

The situation in Durban, where *Indian Opinion* was produced, was little better. I decided to organise the purchase of a piece of land where a farm could be created and *Indian Opinion* could be produced. The early days were difficult since the land was wild and infested with snakes and scorpions. We lived in tents.

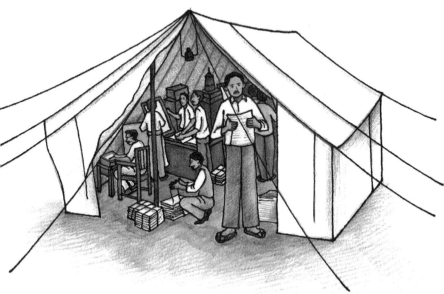

It had been my plan to settle down in Durban, but my work meant I had to return to Johannesburg. It seemed unlikely that I would be able to go back to India for some time, so I asked my wife Kasturbai to join me in Johannesburg.

With her arrival I introduced some household reforms, hoping to train my children to lead a simple life.

'From now on we will make the bread ourselves, and grind the flour too,' I said. 'Everyone will clean up after themselves, including the children.' My children walked with me to work, and I spent a lot of time teaching them. I considered a knowledge of our mother tongue important, and therefore only spoke Gujarati to them.

All the clerks who lived with me were expected to clean their own chamberpots, but a new clerk was ignorant of this and left his dirty.

'I will not clean his chamberpot!' declared Kasturbai.

'Then I will clean it,' I said.

'No,' Kasturbai protested. 'I will not allow you to do that!' She grabbed the pot and cleaned it herself, shedding tears of rage. But I wanted her to do the work happily, and her tears angered me, causing me to scold her. I am ashamed to say that I dragged her out of the house and pulled her towards the gate.

'Have you no shame?' Kasturbai castigated me. Her words brought me to my senses and I let go of her.

My writings in *Indian Opinion* and all my experiences were preparing me for *satyagraha*, the philosophy and practise of nonviolent resistance. I did not immediately find the term to describe it, so sought the help of the readers of *Indian Opinion*. My co-worker, Maganlal Gandhi, suggested a word incorporating *sat* meaning truth and *agraha* meaning firmness; thus *satyagraha* was born.

At this time Kasturbai's health was causing us concern. She was very weak, and the doctor suggested giving her meat. Neither of us was willing to try this, so I suggested giving up salt and pulses instead.

'But you're asking me to give up something that you cannot give up yourself!' retorted Kasturbai.

'In that case I will give up salt and pulses for a year myself!' I declared.

Kasturbai was shocked at my vow, but for me it was an opportunity to test my resolve. We both gave up salt and pulses, and her health improved.

One of my closest friends in South Africa was the German-born architect Hermann Kallenbach. Though he was a rich man and used to luxury, he was strongly influenced by my ideas; he adopted a simple lifestyle and a vegetarian diet. For a time we lived together at Tolstoy Farm – named for the Russian writer who had similar views about simplicity to ours – along with some other families.

Whatever time I could spare, I spent teaching the children. Although I did not believe in beating children, one tested my patience so much that I beat him. The boy understood the pain that had forced me to beat him and was never disobedient again, but I was ashamed of myself and never used violence again. When I next encountered bad behaviour, I fasted, and although this weakened me it made the children who had misbehaved realise their mistake.

In July 1914 my friend Gokhale asked me to join him in England, and so Kasturbai, Kallenbach and I set sail. Kallenbach had expensive binoculars that he used every day on the ship. 'Possessions like that do not match our simple lifestyle,' I told him. 'Why don't you throw them away?'

'I don't mind,' he replied.

I took them from him and threw them into the water. He neither protested nor reproached me, and I was moved by his willingness to change himself and his lifestyle.

We reached London on August 6th, two days after
war was declared against Germany. Gokhale was
stuck in Paris. I was determined to wait for him,
and used the time to meet the Indian community
in London. Most of my countrymen felt that
this was the perfect opportunity to demand our
freedom from the English, but I was certain that
if we helped the English we would win them with
our love. I therefore wrote to Lord Crewe, offering
our team for ambulance work. Although this
participation in war went against my belief in nonviolence, I did it because it was my duty.

I was weakened by the recent fasts I had
undertaken, and when he arrived from Paris
Gokhale was unhappy to find me so weak.

'Drink some milk,' he urged. 'It will improve
your health.'

Drinking milk would mean giving up my
principles, but for how long could I withstand
Gokhale's loving support? After thinking it over I

said to Gokhale, 'Please do not force me to drink milk.' He did not force the issue, but did suggest other ways of improving my health. My health did not improve, however, and I decided that it was time to go back to India. My happiness at going home was reduced by the news that, as a German, Kallenbach was denied permission to leave England.

I did my best to help him obtain permission to travel to India, but the Indian Viceroy sent a telegram saying, 'Regret Government of India not prepared to take any such risk.' It was a great wrench for both of us. If he had come to India he would today have been leading the simple life of a farmer and weaver. Now he is in South Africa, leading his old life and doing brisk business as an architect.

I was warmly welcomed when I landed in Bombay after ten years away from home. In Pune I met Gokhale. He summoned all the members of the Servants of India Society to meet me, and they overwhelmed me with their affection.

I then took the train to Rajkot, where I heard about a 'customs cordon' at Viramgam in the western Indian state of Gujarat, on account of an outbreak of plague. Although an inspection of third class passengers was essential at such times, it seemed to me that the officials made no attempt to hide their contempt for them, treating the poor passengers like sheep. Remembering that Lord Willingdon, the Indian Governor-General, had assured me of help whenever I needed it, I wrote to him, seeking his help; at the same time I supported the protestors in their peaceful protest. The Governor-General's office suggested getting in touch with the Viceroy's office in Delhi. When I met with Lord Chelmsford, the Viceroy, he expressed his astonishment, saying he had known nothing of the matter. He gave me a patient hearing, telephoned for papers about Viramgam, and promised to remove the cordon if the authorities had no explanation for it. Within a few days the cordon had been removed. I regarded this event as the first successful use of *satyagraha* in India.

Shortly after this I heard the sad news of Gokhale's death. It came as a blow to me.

Many people asked me, 'Will there ever be *satyagraha* in India?'

'I have no idea,' I replied. 'I have promised Gokhale to take no decision about how effective it could be until I have travelled widely throughout India and learnt something about my country.' After paying my last respects to Gokhale I set out on my travels. I travelled to Calcutta and from there to Rangoon. I chose to travel third class, and was disgusted afresh both by the indifference of the authorities and by the lack of civic pride among the passengers.

I travelled to Hardvar to participate in the mass Hindu pilgrimage known as the Kumbh Mela, which is held once every twelve years. My work in South Africa had made me a well-known figure, and I found I was constantly being sought out.

At the beginning of 1915 I was looking for a good place near Ahmedabad in the western state of Gujarat to settle the people who had been living in the *satyagraha* farm community in South Africa, and now wanted to come home to India. My dream came true, and in late May we established a farm in Kochrab, a small village near Ahmedabad. We welcomed people from any caste, and within a few months this policy was tested, as a family from the traditionally 'untouchable caste' asked to join the ashram. After much discussion we welcomed them, but several of our supporters stopped funding us as a result. One day I was told that there was no money for the next month. How could the ashram run without funds?

The next day I had a visitor, a man I had met only once before.

'I want to help the ashram,' he said.

'I will gladly accept any help you give me,' I replied.

He was back the next day, this time with thirteen thousand rupees for the ashram. To me this proved that we had made the correct decision in welcoming all classes of Indian society to join our movement.

The fate of Indian indentured labourers in South Africa was once again being discussed, and in March 1916 the Indians moved a resolution in the Imperial Legislative Council to abolish this corrupt and abused system. Many Indians wanted the immediate abolition of the system; the government would only assure them that it would be dealt with in due course. I travelled widely around India, and everywhere I went I saw the enthusiasm of the people for abolition. The government recognised the seriousness of our demands, and the end of the indenture system was announced. This marked the end of a long fight, one that I had begun more than twenty years earlier.

My attention was now drawn to the fate of indigo farmers in Champaran, in the Indian state of Bihar. I visited Patna, the capital of Bihar, for the first time in 1917, and soon realised that there was plenty of work for me to do. The farmers were bound by law to plant three out of every twenty parts of their land with indigo, selling their crop at a fixed rate to their British landowners. 'I am willing to give my time to this cause,' I told the farmers who had come to meet me, 'but I will need your help.'

It was important to find out everything possible about the case, so I decided to meet with the landowners and officials. Instead of receiving their cooperation, however, I was warned that it would be better if I left. I was served with a notice asking me to leave Champaran, and when I refused I was told that I could face criminal charges. Outraged by this threat, thousands of people gathered to demonstrate. The threat was dropped and I was allowed to stay on.

I learnt a lot about the miserable lives of the poor in Bihar during my stay there, and decided that providing schools would be one of the best ways to help them. Volunteers from all over India came to teach in these village schools and to treat the sick. My only sorrow is that after my work was completed most of the volunteers left, allowing nearly all the good work to be lost.

Soon after this I was asked to go back to Ahmedabad and help some mill workers who were asking for higher wages. I suggested that they should go on strike, and that for the strike to be successful they would have to stay firm and not resort to violence.

After a few weeks it seemed to me that they had begun to lose hope. How could I let them give up so easily? What could I do to ensure they went on with their nonviolent action? Suddenly the path became clear to me. 'I will not eat any food,' I announced, 'unless you continue your strike.'

'Forgive us for losing hope,' the workers pleaded. 'We will continue our fight!'

On the first day of my fast some of the workers and their friends joined me. Within three days a settlement was reached for higher wages and the strike was called off.

In the spring of 1918 the people of Kheda, in the Indian state of Rajasthan, were suffering because their crops had failed, creating a state of hunger bordering on famine. They had asked the authorities to be relieved from paying taxes for a year, but their request had been turned down. I explained the concept of *satyagraha* to them, and helped them to draft a petition. The villagers stayed firm in their resolve, and a solution was agreed whereby the poor farmers would be exempted from the tax if the rich farmers paid theirs. It wasn't the best possible outcome, but it proved that *satyagraha* worked.

I was invited by the Viceroy of India to speak at a conference in Delhi in support of the war effort, as more Indian soldiers were needed in the war against Germany. I spoke in Hindi – this was the first time someone had spoken in Hindi at a meeting of this nature. I was shocked that no one seemed willing to listen to me or help me; everywhere I went I was asked the same question, 'As a supporter of *satyagraha*, of nonviolence, how can you work for the war effort?'

The news of Germany's defeat in November 1918 made me glad. It meant I could stop travelling around India recruiting for the war effort, but as a result of my travels I fell ill with dysentery.

Again doctors suggested drinking cow's milk. I explained my reluctance. 'Why not try goat's milk then?' said Kasturbai. The doctor approved, and I began to drink goat's milk. 'I am not happy about drinking goat's milk and breaking my vow,' I told Kasturbai, 'but I am eager to get better and lead people in *satyagraha*.'

To this day I feel ashamed of myself for accepting that goat's milk.

My health improved slowly, and India awoke to the news that Germany had been defeated.

The British government now made a frightful mistake. They decided to follow the suggestions of the Rowlatt Committee, which recommended the extension of wartime restrictions in India, including curfews and the suppression of free speech. I read about the Rowlatt Committee's report and knew that something had to be done.

I wrote to the Viceroy, warning him that if the law was not withdrawn I would launch a campaign of *satyagraha*. Even though my health had still not fully returned, I travelled to Madras, and while I was there the Rowlatt Law was published as an Act. One night the plan to proceed came to me in a dream. 'Let us call for a general strike, or *hartal*, a day on which Indians will suspend all business and purify themselves by fasting and praying.' The *hartal* was held on April 6th 1919, and was very successful.

One of the ways in which the British government in India raised money was from a tax on salt, which I had always believed to be wrong, as salt is a basic ingredient of people's diets. In my book *Hind Swaraj* I had written that the salt tax was a barbarous practice. 'Let us break the salt law,' I suggested. 'People can make salt in their homes. Thousands of copies of *Hind Swaraj* were sold, and the money raised went to help the civil disobdience campaign.

I now travelled to Delhi and Amritsar, but was served with a written order prohibiting my entry into Punjab in the north of India since my presence was likely to disturb the peace. This angered the people of Bombay, and a huge crowd gathered to greet me on my return. The police requested my help in controlling them, but the crowd was too great for my voice to be heard and the police, unable to control the crowd, attacked it.

I was eager to go to Punjab where every day brought fresh reports of the government's atrocities, which included firing on Indians who were taking part in peaceful demonstrations. When I was finally allowed to go to the Punjab, the people gave me a warm welcome. During my stay there I gathered the accounts of the cruelty of the government officials, producing a report which was presented to the government. Rather than punish the officials, however, the government passed an act to protect them from responsibility for their actions. Indian feelings were outraged.

The people of the ashram had always dreamt of dressing in cloth that was handwoven, rather than made in mills. In November 1917 I met a woman called Gangaben, who said she could find us a spinning wheel so we could make our own cloth. She found not one, but hundreds of spinning wheels, and many women told Gangaben that they would spin again if someone supplied the cotton and bought their yarn.

I said that we could promise this, and soon the ashram was receiving more hand-spun yarn than we could cope with. I and many others learnt the art of spinning, and before long *khadi*, cloth made from start to finish by hand, was seen again. Making *khadi* brought precious income to poor landless labourers and the unemployed, and the hand-made cloth offered proof of honest, patriotic labour. Wearing *khadi* quickly became a symbol of dignity and of a bond between lowly and well-off Indians.

I shall stop my account here, as since 1921 my life has been so much in the public sphere that there is hardly any incident that is not known and written about at length. I am still engaged in self-purification, and although I have tried hard I am not yet above feeling love and hatred, attachment and disgust. I beg the reader to pray with me, so that I may be given peace in mind, word and deed.

TAKING THINGS FURTHER

The real read

This *Real Reads* version of *My Experiments with Truth* is a retelling of the original autobiography of Mahatma Gandhi, which covers his life up until 1921. It was first published in Gujarati in weekly instalments between 1925 and 1929; the first English translation appeared in 1940. If you would like to read the full story, many complete editions are available, and you should be able to find a copy in your local library or book shop. The best edition is the authorised version with an introduction by the writer Sissela Bok.

You should be aware that *My Experiments with Truth* ends when Gandhi was 52 years old, and some of the most important campaigns and events he was involved with happened between 1921 and his assassination in 1948.

He spent most of the 1920s in the limelight, but in 1928 he put forward a resolution to make India a semi-independent dominion, and when this was ignored he continued to organise marches against the hated salt tax.

Through the 1930s he continued to work for the rights of the poor, giving special emphasis to women and the 'untouchables', and the British government started to take him seriously, as they could see he was a very popular leader.

When in 1939 Britain assumed that India would unquestioningly join forces against Nazi Germany, many including Gandhi found themselves torn between nonviolence and the need to take a stand against German threats.

India finally achieved independence in August 1947, but Gandhi was shot dead on 30th January 1948 on his way to address a prayer meeting by a man called Nathuram Godse.

Though he was born Mohandas Karamchand Gandhi, he is most often called 'Mahatma' or 'revered one', or affectionately as 'Bapu' or 'father'. His birthday on 2nd October is celebrated as a national holiday in India, while 30th January is known as Martyr's Day.

Filling in the spaces

In compressing *My Experiments with Truth* we have had to leave out many details and stories. The points below will fill in some of the gaps, but nothing can beat the original.

- In 1896 Gandhi volunteered to inspect homes and toilets when plague threatened Rajkot. This opened his eyes to the poor sanitary conditions in the homes of many upper class Indians.

- In 1899 Gandhi gathered Indians to form an Ambulance Corps to fight in the Boer War. He also formed an Indian Ambulance Corps during the Zulu Rebellion.

- While Gandhi was travelling to Natal in 1902 he read John Ruskin's book *Unto this Last*, which gave him the idea to set up the Phoenix Settlement.

- Gandhi nursed his son Manilal to health by giving him baths, wrapping him in a wet sheet, and feeding him orange juice.

- Gandhi first went to jail in 1908, where he learnt to eat without salt or spices. He also learnt that self-imposed restrictions work better than those enforced by others.

Back in time

When Mohandas Gandhi was born in 1869, Europe ruled the world. The colonial powers of Britain, France, Germany, Holland, Spain and Portugal controlled huge territories in Africa, Asia and the Middle East. The British Empire ruled all of India, from present-day Pakistan in the west to present-day Burma in the east; this Indian realm, often called the Raj (raj means 'rule' in Hindi), was seen as the brightest jewel in an empire that also included Canada, Australia, much of Africa, and countless smaller territories.

India was an ancient and in many ways very advanced civilization. The lure of trading with a country known for its spices and silks brought English merchants to India. The first wave of Englishmen who came to India admired Indian culture and languages, which several of them studied in depth.

With the decline of Mughal power in India, the British didn't so much conquer India as fill a power vacuum, first under the auspices of the East India Company, which used British troops to protect and expand its trade, and then after 1857 directly under the British Crown. As time passed, British influence over the kings of India increased, as did their role in the politics of the country. The Battle of Plassey (Palashi) in 1757 was the first decisive victory of the British East India Company. It established Company rule in Bengal, which expanded over much of India over the next hundred years.

As the British administrative control over people's lives in India increased, so did their attempts to mould India and Indians to their needs. Indians became increasingly disturbed at the unwanted interference in the social, cultural and even religious aspects of their lives.

A rumour spread that a new rifle, one that used bullets covered with animal fat, was to be introduced; this was upsetting to the vegetarian *sepoys* – the Indian soldiers – who saw it as indicative of the complete disregard of their religious sentiments. The resulting anger, coupled with growing uneasiness about the greed and unfairness of colonial rule, found release in an uprising in 1857. This uprising, which spread quickly through many towns and villages of northern India, came as a rude shock to the British. The uprising was finally put down in 1858, after which India was ruled by the British government.

The British government required educated people to help run the country, and encouraged the education of Indians. These educated Indians soon became the voice of the nation, making it clear that they were unhappy at being ruled by outsiders. The influence of their traditional belief system remained strong, and often led to conflicts between educated Indians.

This is the India that Gandhi was born into. His initial infatuation with the European way of life was expressed in his desire to dress and look like a European, but he soon understood the importance of following the values he had grown up with and rejected this way of life.

Though Gandhi was a member of the educated class, his distaste of modernity and his love of ancient India set him apart from most of his professional contemporaries. He studied to be a lawyer in England, but never felt comfortable in London and longed to go home. Gandhi believed passionately in the traditional Indian values of abstinence, almsgiving and vegetarianism.

As a lawyer Gandhi travelled to South Africa, where there was a large Indian community but where Indians were treated very much as second class citizens. The time he spent in South Africa opened Gandhi's eyes to the unfairness of racial prejudice. This prompted him to launch a fight for the rights of the Indians in South Africa, and it changed the way he looked at his own homeland. He realised that in order to explore their own destiny, Indians needed to be free of British rule.

His struggle for the truth and his unflinching acceptance of his own weaknesses helped Gandhi perfect the concept of *satyagraha* or 'insistence on truth', which became an important part of his practice of nonviolent resistance.

Finding out more

We recommend the following books, websites and films to gain a greater understanding of Mahatma Gandhi.

Books

- Sandhya Rao and Nilima Sheikh, *Picture Gandhi*, Tulika, 2008.

- Subhadra Sen Gupta, *A Flag, a Song and a Pinch of Salt*, Penguin India, 2007.

- Subhadra Sen Gupta, *Mahatma Gandhi: The Father of the Nation*, Penguin India, 2010.

- *Mahatma Gandhi: Father of the Nation*, Amar Chitra Katha, 2009.

- Shashi Deshpande, *The Narayanpur Incident*, Penguin India, 2013.

Websites

- www.gandhiashramsabarmati.org
Gives information about Gandhi's life, details of his family tree, and a chronology.

- www.mkgandhi.org
A comprehensive website with photographs, selected letters, speeches, and much more.

- www.gandhiserve.org/e/index.htm
View pictures and videos of Gandhi, and listen to him delivering a speech.

- www.mahatma.com/index.php
Has a wide range of information about Gandhi, including a timeline, photographs and speeches.

Films

- *Gandhi*, directed by Richard Attenborough, Sony, 1982. With Ben Kingsley in the title role, this epic film follows his life from the defining moment in 1893 when he is thrown off a South African train for being in a whites-only compartment, and concludes with his assassination and funeral.

Food for thought

Here are some things to think about if you are reading *My Experiments with Truth* alone, or ideas for discussion if you are reading it with friends.

● How far do you think Gandhi was truly aware of his own weaknesses? Do you think that how he struggled to overcome them was the best way?

● Do you think Gandhi was a good father and husband, or did his work always come first?

● How much do you think Gandhi's experiences in South Africa made him aware of the need to fight for independence in India? Could he have done what he did if he had not spent time outside his own country?

● How do you think Gandhi's emphasis on living a simple life changed him? Do you think it made him a better person? Can you think of ways in which you might live a simpler life which would help you be a better person?